Rockin' Him Hard
Omnibus Edition

By

Lynda Belle

Shadowcat Publishing

San Jose, California

Format: Omnibus Edition

Author: Lynda Belle

Cover Design: Visual Effects

Editor: Claudette Cruz

Beta Readers: Alain Gomez and Lisa Frogjourney

ISBN: 0997817003
ISBN-13: 978-0997817003

To all the rock stars that have inspired me:
Adam Ant
Jon Bon Jovi
Simon Le Bon
John Taylor
Brett Michaels
Brendon Urie

CONTENTS

Rockin' Him Hard

Rockin' Him Harder

Rockin' Him Fierce

Rockin' Him Solo
**Bonus sequel story

.

Rockin' Him Hard

Hot Groupies Series Book 1

Chapter 1

"I dare you to get us backstage." I smiled as I faced my best friend Shelly, hands on my hips, staring at her orange and black hair. She had bragged so much about working at a radio station and getting backstage at shows, I was getting to the point that I wanted to see if it was true. "I bet after all that experience in Ohio working for that station will make it pretty easy to get us back there."

She looked at me a moment. Her emerald eyes accented by black eyeliner and lashes I would kill for twinkled with amusement. "You're on."

She grabbed my hand and moved to the front of the stage. The crowd was a bit relaxed for an afternoon music festival. It wasn't a mosh pit fest, and people often made way for pretty girls. Besides, we were heading up during a break in the bands, and that made it easier to weave our way around the people that were leaving.

We made it up at the front in time for the comedian/host/MC to come out. He had a short stint on one of the sitcoms in the 80s, and he was milking those appearances for all it was worth. We made it up to the front, and hung off the wall waiting for the next band to appear.

"Hey, Marty." Shelly called his character's name. I could tell she was milking his drive to be noticed still, even if it was only for being once a child star. He turned to see her and smiled. Her timing was impeccable. She lifted her shirt, right as he turned. The blush from "Boy Marty" told me she'd scored the ultimate get noticed points.

Shelly elbowed me when Marty left. "Now, when the band comes on, you've got to join me."

"You didn't say I was going to have to help to get backstage."

"This is a joint operation. Besides, it's more fun when we're both working the rock stars. Trust me."

That's when the band we'd been waiting for came on. Secret Fire was rising up the charts fast. They had one big hit, and it looked like they were certain for super stardom. This might be the last chance to see them before they started hitting the stadiums.

For me, I loved their raw, edgy sound that grinded you into a passion that made you want to jump on anything that moved. I stared at each member as they entered, remembering them from the music festival poster.

The bassist had these to die for light blue eyes and dark black hair. He wore a tight black t-shirt with a skull, and tight black jeans. He was to my left, with the lead singer to my right. I recognized him from the cover of their album. He gave me a look that drew me in. His long brown hair and angular face started to sway as the band started their first song. He grabbed the mic with both hands, and wailed out the beginning lyrics. His tank top revealed his biceps and dragon tattoo that was the main picture on the back of the album.

Shelly had dragged me to all of this. She had known them back in her days in Ohio. She was so excited they were finally making the big time. Besides, it's harder being a singleton at a concert. That's the one thing about a good friend; they know when they need to help you. She was always the one poking me into action. Once I got started, there was no closing off my wild half.

I started to notice a couple of the stagehands and a few men in suits looking at us from behind the makeshift stage. I think they knew what was coming. Shelly started a countdown. As we came to the chorus, she began, "One, two, three."

We both lifted our tops at the same time. The lead singer joked on the most popular line. The audience took it up thinking he was letting them take over. A smile appeared on his face as we lowered our tops; he began to sing towards us.

"Maybe she didn't understand,
That I was just a man.
My feelings torn from me,
When she cheated to set us free."

He leaned down and grabbed Shelly's hand and sang the last two lines to her. They locked eyes, as the drums took over, and the lead guitarist started a riff. The crowd surged, and he broke away freeing himself from Shelly still staring after him.

We stayed there swaying with the crowd through the next three songs. Every once in a while, I saw Shelly motioning to a guy in a suit backstage. Before I knew it, the band was finished with their set and leaving the stage.

That's when Shelly grabbed my hand so we could ease out of the crowd. The band left the stage. We were walking back to the back stage entrance hoping to catch them in time. Now, the challenge was on.

"OK, you've got to follow my lead now," she said as she walked up to the security guard. There is always one posted no matter what.

"Sure, anything you say. It's a team effort." I was having trouble keeping up; she had made such a sprint once we got out of the crowd.

She straightened her tight skirt walking up to him, licking her lips before she spoke.
"Hi, where are you from?"

The guy was so muscle bound. I could see his veins bulge when he crossed his arms. His t-shirt was so tight it would burst if he moved too quickly. "East Coast. Jersey."

"Umm, I love Jersey men. We don't get many around here. We're in such a small town. There's not much to do, but tip cows."

He was smiling, as he said, "No, I don't imagine you do get much action around here. This county fair set-up is pretty low standards from what we've been used to."

"You know," she moved her arms closer together and lowered her front to show more cleavage, "I was watching backstage and saw a guy motion for us to come back here."

"Sure you did." He pulled his arms more together shaking his head a bit.

She brought herself closer to him, leaned against the fence saying; "I think he's coming up behind you right now."

The sound of footsteps and shoveling made the security guard turn around. "Here you go girls."

A man came from behind the guard and handed Shelly two laminated passes through the fence. She caught them and handed one to me. The security guard shook his head as he opened the gate for us.

Shelly caught the guard around the waist as we walked by. "Too bad you've got to do your job. You look like you'd be a lot of fun."

"Like wise. I'm already jealous of the band."

The man that handed the passes to Shelly had already taken off, and we followed in his direction. I quickly put the pass around my neck and asked, "Who is that?"

"That's the manager of the band. We used to work at the radio station together. I recognized him earlier. We go way back."

We walked through the area roped off, and headed for a tent behind the stage. Set up inside was several food tables and pour yourself alcohol. Several folding chairs were taken up by people already. I weaved my way to an open space and sat down.

Shelly came over to me with a beer in hand. "So, did I win the dare?"

"Yes. I declare you the winner." I looked around marveling that she'd actually done it in less than an hour.

"Come on Michelle, you've got to loosen up. This sure beats studying or writing papers. Sometimes taking a break from classes is a good thing."

I looked at her, a little dumbstruck. It didn't quite feel like me to be hanging out with roadies and behind the scenes at a rock concert. But than, I'd promised myself, college was going to be different. "No, you're right. This is good."

"Hell yeh. A little break in life keeps it sweet."

"Hey girls," I heard a voice say behind me.

I turned and noticed the lead singer, Brandon, of Secret Fire standing behind me. "Want to go to a party?"

Chapter 2

I'd never ridden in a limo before. I was wedged between the drummer and bassist of Sweet Fire enjoying the man scent lingering around me. I could smell the sweat and energy of the stage show still hanging on them. The bassist, Randy I think was his name, kept leaning up against me, and I enjoyed the limited space between us. This was the place to be.

Shelly sat across from me leaning heavily on Brandon. He had his arm wrapped around her and held a beer in the other. On her other side was Jake, the lead guitarist, but he didn't seem to lean into her. Apparently, the rumor was he had a girlfriend.

Brandon tossed me a beer. After catching it, he responded, "Good, you pass the test for quick thinking. I like my women to be fast." He started reaching around Shelly's waist, and pulling her closer. She put her hand on his chest and started caressing through his shirt.

I could tell she'd made her choice for the night. The question was, could I? Randy was nuzzling closer to me, brushing my hair from my face. "You going to take a drink of that Michelle?"

I should give him points for at least remembering my name. "Sure." And I downed half the bottle.

Applause erupted in the limo. "Damn Shelly, you brought us a wild one to play with." Brandon kissed Shelly, and took another swig of beer.

Randy clinked bottles with me. "Can you do that again?"

"Sure." I downed the rest of the bottle, and let out a loud burp. "Nothing to it. You just open wide and swallow." I winked at him and the whole limo broke up laughing.

That's when Randy kissed me. Nothing to write home about, but a definite claim to me among the members of the band. My fate may be sealed for the rest of the evening. I looked back into his blue eyes, black hair framing his face. And I liked what I saw. His smile broadened.

"I think I may need another beer," I said snuggling into Randy.

"Damn, man, get this girl another." The lead guitarist dug in the limo fridge and tossed me another beer.

I answered with another burp. "I might have to go a bit slower on this one. I might have filled my limit for the time being. "

"You can do what you want, babe. The sky's the limit when you're lit on fire." I smiled at the cryptic response from Brandon. He wrote the lyrics for the band. So, I wasn't surprised by his literary metaphor. I had a feeling the fire was only starting. Hopefully, it could end with a full bonfire.

We arrived at their hotel in style. Screaming fans were pushed away by hotel security as we entered the building. Shelly and I were getting looks from envious girls staring us down. After all, we each had a band member draping their arms around us. I felt I'd crossed the ultimate groupie wall.

We paraded through the lobby, and headed straight for the elevator. I downed another beer waiting for the elevator to arrive, and was beginning to feel some after affects. Randy was keeping me up, reaching underneath my black tank top to keep me afloat.

We went up to the 16th floor where the suites were located. One of the members needed to use their key in the elevator to get us to the top. Luckily, one remembered it. I managed to only stumble into Brandon, in which he grabbed my other arm to steady me. There was a big laugh when he said, "At least she knows how to hold her liquor. Walking is another thing."

We shuffled in a stream of arms and legs tangled together down the hall to a room we could hear music was already booming out of. This had to be the After Party.

When the door opened, Brandon led with a huge declaration, "OK everyone, the party can officially begin." There was a cheer from inside as Shelly and I were ushered in with the band. Throughout the room, people mingled with drinks, smoking, and talking.

The den of noise was an assault on my senses, and I excused myself from Randy to go out on the patio. I just wasn't used to all of this happening at once. I was used to frat parties. Beer tricks worked there. But this was a whole other party ball game.

A little after, Shelly followed. "You OK Michelle?"

I shook my head. "Yey, I just needed a break. I think downing the beers has left me a bit light headed. Is there any food in there? It might help."

"Yea, hold on. I'll go see what I can find."

I continued to look off the balcony. The lights from the freeway and downtown stood out among the hills in the distance. It helped settle my head to breath deeply. The fresh, crisp air steadied me. Then, I felt arms wrap around my middle.

"Feeling better, babe?" I recognized Brandon's voice. His warmth enveloped me as the breeze came up. His mouth nuzzled behind my ear and tickled the tip as he kissed it. The beer kept me from my normal reaction. Normally I'd freeze up. But this, in the arms of a rock star, was a whole new experience.

He crept down the back of my neck and I leaned into him. Nuzzling my shoulder, he stroked my belly and crept underneath my tank. Fondling gently, he cupped each breast. I leaned back more as he bent over and kissed the other side of my neck. I was feeling like I was melting under his touch. He was gentler than I thought he'd be.

In fact, there was an amount of surprise he was with me. I couldn't deny the tingles that raced around my middle, and fire developing between my legs. Much more of this and I was going to be sliding all over him, not caring what he did to me.

He continued to grab my right breast, focusing on the sensitive nipple that was springing into action by a man's touch. "You O.K. with this Michelle?"

"Yes, oh god, yes", I whispered leaning back more as he pulled me towards him. His hands continued their climb upward as he wrapped my lips with his. Gentle suction on my mouth made the wetness start between my legs. Brandon's seduction wasn't anything I'd had before. I started to caress under his shirt for the fabulous chest I'd only seen on Internet photos.

I started to stroke his abdomen, caressing up towards his upper chest. He only stopped for a moment to enjoy my explorations, closing his eyes as I claimed new territory, caressing his broad shoulders and masculine neckline.

I was taken out of this dream by his whispered request, "I think I know somewhere that we can go to be more alone. Are you up for it?"

I answered him by pulling him down for another kiss. He grabbed my hand saying, "Come on

Chapter 3

"What about Shelly?" Brandon was leading me down the hall to another room.

"She'll find us if she wants to. Right now, I'm interested in you."

He stopped for a moment to pull me towards him and kiss me. The kiss had a succulent pull that I felt down to my toes. I returned his passion with the same suction showing I learned fast.

"God girl, you are hot," Brandon claimed as he grabbed my ass in my tight black skirt.

"You're a sexy rock god. Why pick me?" I couldn't stop it before it came out.

"I always like the quiet ones. I don't trust the outgoing, wild girls."

"But you said in the limo, you liked wild women." I wrapped my arms around his neck.

He bent down and whispered in my ear, "It's the wild ones that hurt you the most."
He had a lost look in his eyes, than changed the subject. "But, I know how to bring out the wild side of a woman. I know how to push buttons to release her."

He led me to a room near the end of the hall, put in a key card, and pulled me to him. As we went in, he shut the door with his foot. Then, he cupped my chin and kissed me. This time, there was a hunger I hadn't felt before. Something carnal was building within me. I wanted him to stroke me in all the right places. I was feeling the need for him to strip me of clothes.

I crept under his t-shirt again as he pulled it over his head, throwing it to the other side of the room.

He cradled my face as he asked, "What do you want Michelle?"

"I want you to bring out my wild side."

He stroked my body down to my waist, and pulled my tank top over my head. The feeling of liberation was transporting me to another place. The wild Michelle was emerging. He caressed my nipples again bringing them to life. My back arched in his arms as he held me up. I felt the wildness build within. He lowered me onto the bed hovering over me, kissing down my stomach.

"Are you ready?" He looked me in the eyes, a gentle teasing glint as he stared with avid desire. But, I sensed it was up to me to give the go ahead. I could back out. This was my moment. How hard did I want to rock him?

"Release me Brandon." I was his for the taking. He pulled off my skirt, with just my panties, wet with longing, keeping me from him. He pulled those off next, with just my inner recesses ready to receive what he had to give. He licked down around my nipples, sucking deep one then the other. Grabbing my breast, he stroked with his other hand down my belly feeling his way down to my thighs.

My body responded to his touch, arching my back as he found my wet opening. He began to stroke my clit, slow and steady, grabbing my breast at the same time. "Come for me Michelle." I gasped as he pushed his fingers deeper, moving them quicker and quicker over my clit until I was in agony to come.

I burst with the pleasure waves of my orgasm shuttering through my body. Not one wave, but several until I was spent. I was surprised at how much he'd built my lust.

Brandon was poised above me. "Are you ready for more?"

My raspy "Yes" gave him the go ahead to continue the rapture. He stood up and slid off his jeans. But I couldn't let the next part be done alone. It was my turn to rock him. I sat up before he could take his underwear off. Sitting up to match his eyes, I pulled down to release his large rod. I cradled his member in my hands, stroking it into a large mammoth monster.

His shaft felt like silk as I rubbed the tip. I was satisfied by his shudder. "God Michelle, it didn't take long to release your wild side." I placed my mouth over the top, rounding my lips into the perfect "O". I slid my mouth up and down listening to the moan that escaped Brandon's lips. He placed his hand behind my head, guiding my mouth to not stop. I had no intention to until he was ready to bury himself inside me.

I stopped and looked into his eyes. "I want you inside me, but..." I held his shaft, holding it ready for a sheath of protection.

His labored breath stumbled over the words. "There's one in my jeans pocket."

I crawled to the floor, digging through the jeans. I retrieved the condom, and ripped it from its package.

"Look, ribbed for my pleasure." Standing next to him, I grabbed his cock again, and rolled over the protection.

Brandon eased me back on the bed, kicking his underwear completely off and flinging them against the wall. He couldn't hold himself back much longer. He nestled his fingers back inside me, drawing the wetness out, and sending my snatch into a creamy frenzy.

"Do you want me?" Brandon's breath blew against my ear with his urgent request.

"First, I want to hear that I'm your number one groupie."

"Yes. You are the incarnation of my wildest groupie."

"Then, fuck me hard Brandon. I want you inside me."

He plunged deep within my folds. I wrapped my legs around him as he thrust again and again. I arched with each thrust, opening wide for him to bury himself within me. Our ecstasy built until neither one of us could hold on any longer. Brandon made a last thrust, and waves of sensual pleasure rolled through me again as we came together.

"Can anybody come play?"

I had little chance to move from what had just rocked my body. But I recognized Shelly's voice. A panic erupted in my gut. Brandon remained laying on top of me, putting his fingers over my lips. "It's ok. She's joining us."

Shelly walked in the bedroom door, her arm extending onto the frame. "Well, looks like I interrupted something. Can I join too?"

Brandon looked at me. "It's up to Michelle. Can she?"

Before I could answer, Shelly walked over beside the bed, her tank already discarded in the living room, with only her panties still on. "You know Michelle, the best way to bond with your friends is to share a man."

I must have been dumbfounded. The glow of Brandon's lust still was on me, and I was stark naked. I felt vulnerable. "I'm not sure Shelly. I've never done that before."

"No problem. We can do this tag team style. I'm tagging you out Michelle. Now, it's my turn to rock'im."

She held up her hand for a high five, and I got up sitting back in one of the easy chairs in the room. I leaned back and watched as Shelly crawled to the bed. Brandon rolled onto his back. His face was eating up the sight of Shelly. She lay across him, gliding her panties down off her legs. Then, sat up, straddling him. He couldn't keep his hands off her.

Brandon reached up, squeezing Shelly's breast as she leaned back. Her hair cascaded behind her as she rocked back and forth over his member. The rubbing was creating his cock to grow again. Shelly leaned down on him, her cunt directly kissing his cock, rubbing her juices along his shaft. His pole sprang back into action. She continued building their sensuous connection, rubbing and leaning down finally to ease his shaft into her.

Then, she pumped him. Again and again she was smacking him hard as she rode him into a state of delirium. He begged for her to keep going. Shelly leaned back, keeping her balance as she bucked with the stallion of a rock star beneath her. Finally, they climaxed together, with moans of rapture as she collapsed on top of him. After a moment, she kissed him. His state of pure bliss left him a lump on the bed. She carefully rolled off him, and went into the bathroom.

I followed her. She was cleaning up and tossed me a towel. "Time to go. Brandon is going to be out of it for awhile."

She held up her hand for another high five. "I think you're in."

"What do you mean?"

"Sweet Fire is one of the bands I knew from hanging out at the radio station. There's a whole group of special groupies that prefer to hang out with the band after hours. I think you've made the grade to be one of us."

"You mean there's more girls that do the band members."

"Well, they have their special groupies. I'm one of Brandon's. It's a select club. I think he's chosen you too. You up for it?"

I thought of Brandon's chest, his masculine smell, and his cock in my hands. "Yes. I'm up for this. What do I have to do?"

She finished, and threw the towel in the tub. In the living room, she went about picking up her clothes, and found some of mine.

"I've got our backstage passes for the next show." She handed me my tank. "We can ride on the bus with the band or meet them later. You're definitely in, right?"

"You have so won the dare, Shelly." I went and gave her a big hug. "This was better than anything!"

"Well, I don't just bring the band just anyone. I only bring them awesome, gorgeous chicks to hang with. Spring break is next week. So, we can join them in a few days."

"So, you in?" Her eyes looked at me waiting for an answer.

It was the second time I would step into the wild side. "Yes, absolutely yes."

Rockin' Him Harder

Hot Groupies # 2

Chapter 1

Shelly and I proudly wore our backstage passes. We skirted the crowd at the back of the club waiting for Sweet Fire to start their set. After throwing some overnight bags into Shelly's car, we'd rushed down to grab the Greyhound bus to get to the next town on the tour. Shelly was banking on the fact we were promised a ride on the tour bus after we caught up. After all day on the bus, I was ready for a drink.

The warm-up band was in full swing pumping the crowd into a frenzy of anticipation.

"This opening band rocks! I'm going up to the front." Shelly pulled me forward to weave between the less than die hard fans as we crashed our way through to the front.

I could follow easily behind Shelly's orange black tipped hair as she slid through cracks between people. The lead guitarist was in a rage riff, and I watched the crowd follow along in full head banging mode. This was going to turn into a pit of crushing bodies. I hoped Shelly knew what she was doing.

"Hey babe, where you going?" Some guy asked me as I got shoved into him.

"Sorry." It was all I had time to say as Shelly pulled me away.

"Brandon is way cuter. Don't waste your time on fans Michelle."

The crowd started to ease closer, and openings where harder to find. We finally edged up behind some girls just as the opening band finished. Shelly recognized a girl and went up behind her.

"Tia!" Shelly yelled for the attention of the girl. As the band left, Tia turned around, her pink hair swinging into a woman next to her. "Girl, how you been?" Tia jumped on Shelly wrapping her arms around her.

Just at that moment, the warm up band finished. "Thanks, mother fuckers! Sweet Fire will be on next." The crowd roared at the announcement. Michelle and I joined in the screaming.

The crowd started to break apart as everyone went to refuel with drinks or take a break before Sweet Fire headed onto the stage.

I watched Shelly wrap herself around the strange girl as she said, "Fabulous. I see you've got our section in reserve."

Tia grabbed a drink sitting on the stage. "Yes. As usual Shelly." She turned to me, and pointed. "Who's your friend?"

Shelly grabbed me and pulled me forward. "This is Michelle. She's been initiated as a groupie at the last gig."

Tia looked me up and down. It was like I was passing an inspection. "Whose groupie is she?" She held the straw of her drink, biting the end.

"Brandon's." Shelly high-fived me.

Tia sucked more of her drink through the straw. "I bet you gave him what he deserves." She began mouthing the straw, and laughed. "He's the baddest boy in the band."

"What've you been doing?" asked Shelly.

"You know, not much. Hanging out with Sweet Fire on as much of the tour as possible."

"You flying solo?" Shelly had a ring of mischief in her voice.

"Yup. I like it better that way." Tia continued with another drink. "I'm done with my skank of a girlfriend. From now on, I belong to my Sweet Fire boys." Her smile implied volumes of past mischief.

"So girls," a man spoke from the stage as he was setting up the front mic for Brandon. His Irish accent rolled off his tongue in a sexy manner. "Be careful of how much you lean here. And watch the drinks too. We want to stay good with the club, you know."

"No problem Pete," Shelly answered easily. "We know the drill."

"I know you do, but every night it's the same ole' thing. You make me have to pick glass out of your arm again Tia, and I'm going to be pissed."

"Sure, sure Pete. I'll stay out of trouble." She drank again, licking her red lips, and smiled back with the innocent look people do when likely to do something again. She blew a kiss to him, and he waved at her as he walked off the stage.

Tia turned back to us. "So, you just caught up with the band? You're with us for the rest of the tour?"

"I'm hoping so." Shelly flipped a piece of orange hair out of her eyes. "I think the band is cool with us bumming along for the next few towns. That's what Brandon mentioned at the last show."

"Good, I was starting to get lonely for company." She grabbed Shelly's hand. "What's your friend's name?"

"This is Michelle." I smiled back as Shelly motioned to me.

"You ever been a groupie before?" Tia's eyebrow went up as she looked me over.

"No, this is a whole new experience. I'm glad I could arrange to redo my midterms at another time. It frees me up for at least a week."

Tia wrapped her arm around Shelly. "You think we'll be able to blow her mind in a week?"

Shelly laughed. She didn't have a chance to answer. Sweet Fire came running onto the stage, and the crowd went wild. Tia and Shelly braced themselves against the stage, pulling me between them. All of Sweet Fire was there. Their drummer started a beat, and the place went crazy.

We started moving to the beat just as the bassist Randy started his run. He drove into the guitar, fingering some bass lines that got me pumping my arms, and then he looked at me. He smiled, recognizing me instantly.
I remembered our kiss in the limo, and was happy that I'd hooked up with Brandon instead. Randy had gorgeous blue eyes, but Brandon had the rock god body that was a fan's wet dream.

The band got the crowd revved up for Brandon's entrance. He strolled onto the stage, his body wrapped up in a leather jacket, his brown hair loose about his shoulder, and a cat grin wrapped onto his face. Brandon stepped near the front of the stage. He stared at the crowd slowly, taking them in. Then, Jake, the lead guitarist, struck the first chord of their intro song. The crowd moved into us, pushing us against the stage.

Brandon launched into the lyrics of their popular hit on the charts, making me sway and move to his sexy voice. I could remember his hands caressing me, just as his voice was now. I swayed, closing my eyes, hearing his voice remind me of his tongue gliding down my stomach. My thighs felt an ache between them. And there was more wetness than just sweat rolling through my naughty bits. Would he want to take me again like he did at the last show? I wasn't sure I'd be able to say no.

He bent down, and sang the lyrics of the song.

"Come to me, and let me love you
Down to the floor,
Let me take you.
Slowly, more and more
Let me rule you.
I promise
To cherish you."

I was locked into Brandon's eyes. His sweat filling my senses. My heart beating for him to take me again. Our spell was broken by Tia and Shelly screaming on either side of me. Brandon smiled, reached under my chin, and stroked my cheek.

To everyone else, it looked like a lovesick fan worshipping their idol. For me, it was a promise of being taken by Brandon again. And this time, I wanted to give him everything.

Chapter 2

I held the glass of champagne backstage waiting for the rest of the group to come into the room. We had ushered ourselves backstage before the end of the show, and were in full pounce mode for when they came through the door. I balanced my wine glass with my other hand, turning my foot in a needless shuffle of my toe. Would they hurry up now? This was the third encore, and I was becoming impatient. Or was I just demanding? Was I able to keep my hands off Brandon much longer? He kept singing to me through the whole set, and I was mad to rip his tank off by the end of the show.

I heard the back stage door slam backwards, and the band barged through with Brandon leading the way. "That's the way to do it! Leave'em wanting more." He fist pumped the air, and went to the buffet table for some food. I watched him saunter around the room, first to talk to Pete and then looking around to spot someone. The someone was me.

The moment he laid his eyes on me, his smile lit up the room. It's all I needed to head towards him. Shelly had gone off in the corner with Tia, draping themselves over Randy when he came in. He had both of his arms full. I'd say he was going to be occupied for the moment. That left Brandon for me.

I sauntered to him, pulling a sip from my drink so my lips would taste of it. The bubbles popped under my nose as he walked towards me. I smelled the tangy, dry taste of the champagne as he pulled me towards him.

"I've been wanting you all night." His voice tingled sensations down my spine.

After missing his touch for the last few days, I was finally where I wanted to be. I answered his plea for more with my lips pressing against his. The champagne taste mingled with his mouth as his tongue connected with mine. Shocks down my back traveled to my thighs. He grabbed me, pulling me closer, spilling champagne onto his shoulder. His dragon tattoo was awash with the champagne. I licked it, tasting the tangy salt of his skin. That's when I felt someone pull us apart.

"Wow Michelle. Leave some for Tia and me."
Shelly wrapped her arms around his waist and
mine. She took the center between us. "Or
maybe we should get a room."

"You bet. I want all of my hot groupies around
me tonight. Get some drinks, girls. I'm glad you
could make the show." He looked over to me.
He mouthed the words "later". I air kissed back
as Shelly pulled Brandon towards Tia.

"Easy girls, there's plenty of me to go around."
Brandon's voice held bemused humor as Tia
started easing her hands up his back under his
tank. He held his hands up as in protest like he
was giving in.

"The question is will you last that long without
us." Shelly joked back.

"Seriously guys, get a room." Shouted Jake from
the other side of the buffet table. "Or at least
wait until we've left."

The girls just looked at him, laughed, and
continued pawing Brandon into a frenzy. I
wanted to join them, but too many eyes were
making me nervous. I wasn't ready to show any
of my lust for Brandon so publicly. Maybe I had
a lot to learn as a groupie.

"This much adoration is going to kill me."
Brandon grabbed each girl pulling them on
either side of him. More people were coming
into the room to have drinks and eat from the
buffet. I watched Shelly and Tia hang off of
Brandon as people came up to talk to him about
the show.

I stayed back, basking in the glory of seeing him
again. My secret rock star lover was a god
among men. His leather pants and black tank
accented his dragon tattoo, his brown hair falling
around framing his face. His angular jawline had
a black shadow that I wanted to rub my hand
across and feel the rough texture. He was
beyond hot. He would burn me like a volcano if
I let him.

The crowd grew around him, and I saw them
part as he moved out of it. Tia and Shelly
followed behind. He stopped in front of me,
grabbed my glass, and drank more champagne.
"You up to an after party?" Then, he kissed me
like the other night. He pulled on my upper lips,
the suction sending sensations down to my toes.
My crouch was lighting up. I wrapped my arms
around him as he pulled me closer.

I came up for air with his answer. "I thought
you'd never ask."

Chapter 3

We clung to him as we stumbled into the hotel room. We were a mass of flesh jackets covering his hot, tattooed body. All I wanted to do was feel every part of his hot ass, and feel him take me again. I wasn't sure I wanted to share him with Shelly and Tia. I tried to keep the jealousy down. Where were these feelings coming from? Shelly had gotten me backstage in the first place. I should allow it all to happen, but for some reason, I wanted Brandon all to myself. I was such a selfish hot bitch right now.

I backed up to the side as Tia and Shelly pushed and pulled Brandon towards the bed. They took off his leather jacket, his bare chest hard and sculptured as they traced his curves. They grabbed each one of his arms and pulled him onto the bed. They started to edge towards him. Lying back, he opened his arms inviting both of my friends to cuddle into them. Brandon looked at me. "I need a top layer Michelle."

"That's ok. I'll watch for now." Again, what was wrong with me? My legs were already getting weak looking at his abs and biceps as he caressed my friends. I slinked into the easy chair in the corner, thinking that if they had they're fun first, I could pounce at the right time and have him all to myself.

They took up either side of him, stripping him down, removing his tank and then his jeans. Socks flew and hit the walls. Other articles of clothing flew off hitting the table, lamp, or ending on the side of the bed. Shelly and Tia helped each other undress in front of him, standing on the bed to do a striptease. They removed each other's bras, dancing to their own beat, shaking their hips and asses pointing towards Brandon. They were groupie sisters, rockin' out making sure Brandon got hard.

Tia had on a pink lace thong while Shelly had on a red one. Brandon was taking in every inch of their groupie bodies, watching their breasts shake up and down, bouncing in rhythm to their inner beat. Finally, he couldn't take it anymore. "Girls, I need your attention, please. Before I burst my balls."

They fell down to either side of him like cats ready to attack their prey. They began their attention with slow stroking. Shelly took the upper half of Brandon. Tia began her ministrations on his hard cock. Kissing him at one end, and stroking him at the other brought Brandon to an unbearable height of pleasure. I tried to hold back my own heat, but could feel the wetness soaking into my panties. I wanted to throw my clothes off, but was mesmerized by the look on Brandon's face.

It was twisted into a beautiful look of passion. His need grew by the stroking of Tia's hand, up and down his cock. I watched the growth of their progress. Shelly kissed his nipples, gliding her tongue along his chest. I remembered the salty tang I'd felt earlier in the night. I leaned forward in the chair, watching Brandon ready to come.

Tia slid down, ready to take all of his throbbing muscle into her mouth. Shelly went to grab something out of her purse, handing it to Tia, as she sucked Brandon's pole in and out. Faster she sucked, until he shouted, "God, I'm going to come."

Tia took a bottle from Shelly, and held it up for me to see. "Cinnamon flavored, my favorite. Makes him extra hot." I was starting to feel this was for my benefit. A lesson for the new groupie. She switched to her hands, lubing his cock with the new flavor. Her hands rubbed up and down, building Brandon to the breaking point. She pointed him up as he came, a fountain of lust spilling over her hands. She went down on him to lick up the product of their lust. "Hmm, my favorite flavor." She laughed.

Both the girls looked at me as Brandon moaned the end of his orgasm. Shelly spoke first. "Now it's your turn Michelle."

They both eased towards me with a glint of mischief in their eyes. Each of my friends grabbed an arm, pulling me towards the bed. Brandon started to revive. My captivity got his attention. He sat up on one arm to watch each of them start to remove an article of my clothing. Shelly pulled off my shirt while Tia pulled down my skirt. I was presented to Brandon in panties and bra, both girls pushing me forward. Then, they jumped on the bed.

Motioning for me to join them, I did the same. We all took a corner as Brandon layed on his side to watch our dancing threesome. I got lost in the freedom of movement, rockin' out for Brandon's eyes. I didn't care who was watching now, even among friends. Then, Shelly stopped. "Michelle, it's your turn now. Strip, girl." They bounced off, Brandon still eyeing me. I had the bed stage.

I started out slow moving my hips back and forth before I reached behind my back and snapped open my bra. I flung it hitting the TV in front of us. My breasts sprung out, bouncing to my movements as I started slipping my panties down one leg and off. Then, I slid it down the other. I snapped my panties to smack against the wall.

My friends slinked back onto the bed towards me. They leaned up pulling me down onto Brandon. He didn't move, but was a willing receiver of what was to come from his groupies. Shelly pulled me to put myself over the top of Brandon. Each of them took up a side as I started to lower myself onto his dick for a crouch kiss from my inner recesses.

Thought was becoming difficult as I started to wet up from the contact of Brandon. I'd waited so long to finally have him. I fell back on him, kissing him deeply, slipping my tongue into his mouth as he kissed me back. He grabbed me, wrapping his arms around my back and flipped me.

"I've been waiting all evening for you Michelle." He leaned downward, kissing me again. He grabbed my lips into his mouth with the suction move I loved. He leaned back; sliding his hands down my breasts and my sides until he was near my clit. His mouth took me in.

I saw my new friends each take a breast, and began sucking on a nipple. I closed my eyes to the sensation of being serviced for the first time. My breasts were massaged and suckled by one as my clit was sucked on by someone else. Then, I felt fingers manipulating my wet vaginal lips. I gasped as someone's fingers felt their way inside me. My nipples were teased with long grabs tweaking the tops.
Keeping my eyes closed, I concentrated on the sensations of being suckled and stroked. Everything was building inside me. A massive explosion was about to be released. The volcano I'd imagined earlier was going to explode. I came so hard. Harder than I'd ever had before.

I opened my eyes to see a circle of smiles. The girls left my sides as they started towards each other.

Then, Brandon started again. I lost all visuals of Shelly and Tia. My eyes were only for Brandon as they left the room. He stroked my clit. The lips of my pussy expanded into a flower to receive his cock. He leaned onto me, kissing my breasts, bringing the sensations back. He licked down between my breasts and down my navel. Sucking on my belly button, he left it with a kiss before moving down towards my wetness between my legs.

I wanted more. I wanted him inside me. I was not beyond pleading. "Brandon, please, fuck me now. I've been waiting all night to have you inside me."

He looked up with a smile as I writhed in exotic torture. He leaned up, and positioned his cock so I could see him. Then, lowering to me, he rubbed his man's head against my opening teasing with quick thrusts inward. Each was a shock to my body building my ecstasy. "All the way Brandon. I want you completely inside me."

He grabbed my thigh and plunged within my folds. The feeling of him inside me rocked to my being. I shuddered as he thrust in me again, and again. Each entry built me higher and higher. He was a rockstar porn god as he brought me to my peak.

I let loose as I felt him join me as we released into each other. A million shocks of pleasure seared my body turning me into a puddle of lust. I lay full with Brandon inside me until he pulled out to lie next to me.

Brandon wrapped his arms around me. I spooned next to him feeling safe and secure in his arms. This is where I'd wanted to be all night. In his arms, I felt completely his groupie. "I'm yours, Brandon. Your number one groupie."

"I know. It's you that I've wanted all night Michelle. You turn me on like no one before. I want you to go with us the rest of the tour."

"How long will that be?" I tried not to think of the midterms I'd promised to make-up.

"3 more weeks."

Fuck midterms. "Yes." I turned towards him and kissed him. I was going to be the best, damn groupie ever.

Rockin' Him Fierce

Hot Groupies Series Book 3

Chapter 1

The Sweet Fire tour bus was crowded with the band members, and the few groupies that were privileged to go along with them to the next town. Lucky for me, I was one of them. I was one of Brandon's favorites. Sticking by him, I found myself sitting in his lap, arms wrapped around his neck swigging beer from the bottle he held to me. I was living pretty in his arms.

I was on the tour bus heading with him on the last week of his tour. The problem was I had to share him with my friend Shelly and other partner in crime groupie, Tia. It's not how I'd dreamed a groupie would be, but at least I had Brandon's attention right now.

I swigged from the bottle, and decided I wanted to stake my territory early on this leg of the tour. Brandon was going to be mine. I just had to convince him that I was the only groupie he'd ever want. His hands lowered down around my waist, and I spied a perfect move.

Pulling myself in, I got his attention with my breasts pressed against his chin. The tight black tank barely held them in while I positioned myself with either leg on the sides of him. He put the bottle down, and moved his hands to cup my butt.

"What are you up to?" His eyebrow went up in the cute way when he knew I was turning into my wild self.

"I want your attention for a moment."

"And you've got it."

I leaned down and whispered in his ear "I want you all to myself after the show tonight."

"And this will be worth my while because…" He grabbed my ass, pulling me closer.

I leaned and whispered again to him "I'll rock you so fierce you'll beg me to do it all again tomorrow." Before he could answer, I smothered him with a kiss. The suction he returned was the perfection I'd learned to do right back at him. I came up for air. In taking a deep breath, I said, "So, you think you can handle my wild side unleashed?"

"Are you kidding? I was hoping you'd come out to play like this. In fact, I've been waiting for it." He kissed me fiercely. Our mouths wrapped in tongue play when I heard Shelly behind us say, "Now, save some for the rest of us Michelle."

I turned to her, hating the interruption. I'd had my chance to see if Brandon was willing to go solo tonight. I was hoping she'd not butt in. "Not yet. I'm not done with him."

"Oh, you playing rough, huh? Don't wear him out before the show. The manager will throw us off the bus. Groupies can't be that distracting."

I turned back to Brandon. "I'll get him all warmed up for the crowd." I bent down to kiss him and Brandon locked onto my lips when I felt a pull from behind. It was the manager this time.

"Knock it off. You can't get the boys all riled up before the show." He pulled me off Brandon's lap, and shuttled us to the back of the bus. "You should have listened to your friend. If you want to stay on, wait until after the show."

I felt like saluting the guy. He walked back to the front and sat in the front passenger seat. I suppressed my need to giggle, and then couldn't hold back. Both Shelley and I let loose in a big girl howl-a-thon.

Randy, the bassist, did salute Pete as he moved to the front. "That's telling him Pete. Keep those girls in line. No hanky panky before the show. But afterwards, you can knock your cocks into whatever you like."

We couldn't hold it back then. Shelly and I lost it. Holding onto each other, we slid down the wall to the bench seat.

"Here's another beer. It should help shut you both up." Jake, the lead guitarist, handed us a cold one, and we clinked bottles. "To the groupie life. Never mind what happens after the show. Just make sure they are ready to go before."

I bonked my bottle back at Randy. "It's a groupie's job."

***

I watched the band from the sidelines backstage. Randy, the tough bassist, with the deep blue eyes gave me a stare through his black bangs. I still loved the way they would fall onto his face when he played. Bass players were always so much hotter when they were the darker brooding band member.

Jake, the lead guitarist usually ignored my efforts to stare him down. He was a showman, playing the crowd, and usually didn't give groupies any mind. He was actually true to his girlfriend.

Then there was Brandon. I watched the gorgeous lead singer of Sweet Fire, singing his heart to the crowd. His back was to me as he raised the microphone in the air, revving the crowd to the fist-pumping beat. He had been beyond my dreams three weeks ago. I'd just been a fan out in the crowd at a concert. Now, I was rockin' him after the shows.

With luck, I was starting to be his number one groupie. He seemed to prefer me to the other two. Tia, the sassy girl we'd picked up in a small town on the way to the bigger stadium shows was up for anything. Shelly, my best friend, had dragged me into the whole world of being a groupie. They were showing me the ways to please Brandon the most.

The thing was, they seemed to have something for each other too. I was playing along for the fun of it. Ménage foreplay was having its advantages. But my eyes had always been for Brandon. He was the fire in my eyes.

I watched him fist-pump the air, getting the crowd to clap with him. They were on their last song of the set, ending with a bang of a finale. The place was shaking from the beat. I could see the front row of girls screaming and reaching towards Brandon. It was not that long ago that I had been one of them.

Ace, the drummer, stood up in front of the drums. It was his classic ending. He pounded hard sending the pumped crowd to a crescendo as they sensed the end of the show. He hit the final beat, and the stage went dark. Then, the lights came on for a moment.

"Thanks everyone for a fantastic night. You are the best! Everyone in Sweet Fire wishes the best for every fucking one of you. Go home; rock each other hard in our name. Good night!"

The band came running off in my direction. I waited for Brandon to come to me. I saw him shake the hands of some of the girls up front. Finally, he rushed towards me, grabbing me in his arms.

"God, that was fucking fantastic. Did you hear them? This has been the best show yet." He kissed me, pulling on my lips in the way that melted my heart our first night. "I feel like I'm on fire."

Randy ran past us. "Bran, time for the encore. They're going to tear this place down if we don't."

Brandon kissed me again. "I'll be back." He rushed back onstage.
I didn't need to say anything. I knew he'd come back to me and I'd be in his arms again soon enough. So far, Shelly and Tia were nowhere to be found. Totally MIA. They had stopped watching the show several days ago. They had taken to hanging out in the green room these days. But I loved watching the guys perform. The music still beat within me, driving me into a passion that I loved to take in from the side of the stage.

I would just dance sometimes too. I'd catch Brandon watching me with a glance. Then, I'd just dance harder. I knew he had to pay attention to the crowd, but it became a game to see how many times I could get him to look at me.

I played that game now. I started swinging my hips to the encore song. If I just lost myself in the dance, I usually got his attention. I swung my hair around to the beat, lost in the song. When I got to a stopping point, I looked up. I met Brandon's eyes for a moment. He smiled and turned back to the crowd.

The song gyrated to its final beats. The college stadium was awash with screams.

"Thanks again everyone. We'll never forget tonight!" Brendon's voice echoed off the stadium walls awash with cheers.

This time, the boys came off to stay. I let Brandon wrap his arm around me, sweat dripping from his shoulders. It didn't bother me. I liked being covered by his musky scent. I knew by now that this was the way he claimed me every night. After two weeks, his claim had been staked without any other band members interfering. But he still did it. I think he liked to signal I was still his.

It made me feel proud that he wanted me. We walked down the back of the stage to the hall that led to the green room. I handed Brandon a towel. Something I'd started doing the second week. If I watched from backstage, I wanted to be useful.

He wiped his face with it and carried it through the door. We arrived as everyone gathered around the room to meet the band, eating from the food table, and having drinks. The normal Sweet Fire after-party had begun.

Tia and Shelley were wrapped into drinking beer and talking to some of the stagehands. I think Shelley had her eye on one. Three weeks with the band seemed to get her drifting to other interests. I was happy to see her veering away from Brandon. I wanted to make him all mine. I was getting tired of sharing.

"Is this a fucking party or not? Let's take it up a level!" Brandon yelled to get people excited that the band had arrived. He loved to get people revved when the band entered the room. He was a living, breathing essence of any front man of a band. People liked to swarm around him. I stayed tucked under his arm, in the eye of the storm.

People came up and gave him fist bumps. "Good show Brandon," one amazed fan said to him. He had the dazzled eye of a guy wanting to be in Brandon's place.

"Thanks bro. You play?"

"Yeah. A little bass."

"Maybe we could jam sometime. Thanks for coming out. You get a drink yet?"

The fan shook his head. "Nah. But I'd love one."

Brandon patted him on the back with his other arm. "Help yourself, man. Mi casa es su casa."

The fan did Brandon's bidding with a strange smile of awe on his face. I knew how hard it was to refuse Brandon. His enthusiasm was infectious.

We made the rounds, Brandon signing t-shirts, shaking hands, and giving hugs to the diehard fans that had backstage passes. I'd been among them just a few weeks ago. I unwound myself from Brandon and let him get to meeting them. I'd learned to get out of the frenzy so he could be all theirs. After all, they were the bread and butter of the band operation. And to his credit, Brandon always wanted to give them his full attention.

I stood back and watched. One heavy-breasted fan bent forward for him to sign her breasts. He took way too much delight in that action. I felt myself purse my lips in jealousy that I buried deep. I was trying not to be protective of him as my man. I did share him with fans, and the select groupies he let into his sphere. But it was hard. I was really wanting to share him less and less.

"Is Brandon visiting with the public again?" It was Tia behind me. Her pink hair bob and burgundy lipstick always made her stand out.

"Yeah. That girl let him sign her tits." I pointed the culprit out to her.

"Don't worry, honey. We both know where he'll be later. You'll feel better when he's sucking yours. What you do with him is only in her dreams."

I watched the girl getting her chest signed as Tia whispered in my ear, "I know you like it. Besides, I know a way to draw his attention away from her."

"And that would be?" I smiled back at her.

She answered with a grab behind me, cupping each breast, and nibbling the back of my neck. I leaned into her as she caressed down my stomach. She knew how to get me started. She pulled my hair back, bending me back towards her into a kiss. Her kisses were sweeter than Brandon's. Small and wet, her lips sucked on mine as we wrapped ourselves around each other. Sucking on her lower lip, she nipped at mine, and our eyes locked.

"You are a sexy vixen when you want to be, Michelle. Do you really want to stay with Brandon forever?"

"I think you're the extra sugar to our cake Tia. Shelley, me, you, and Brandon. We mix well together." OK. It was a bit of a fib. I wanted Brandon all to myself really. But the girl knew how to kiss. I was learning a lot in the School of Groupies from her.

"You know, we can keep each other happy while Brandon dallies with others." She reached down, and poked up into my crotch. I'm sure she felt the wetness beginning.

"You can get me totally hot, Tia. I'll admit. But Brandon really sends me over the edge."

She smiled at me. "Then I'll get you ready for him." She took me in another kiss, suctioning and pulling me towards her.

"Girls, save some of that for me." We stopped to see Brandon had come over to us.

"We were getting ready for you, Brandon" I laughed as Tia grabbed my butt. She had a disappointed look. "You want to join in our fun?"

Brandon grabbed me and pulled me towards him. His kiss took my breath away. I lost myself in his kiss letting his lips suck and moisten at will again and again. When we pulled away, I couldn't help but sigh.

"You two are coming with me now." Each of us grabbed one of Brandon's arms, and let him lead us down the hall to the limo. Both Tia and I snuck a smile to each other. We knew that we'd won the battle between the fans and groupies. It was the one thing that separated us. We could lead Brandon by his dick. The promise of what would happen between us all later was the invitation to leave the after-party. I smiled thinking what would happen next. I couldn't wait.

Chapter 2

Shelley was nowhere to be found. Who knows where she had gone. It was just Brandon, Tia and me. We were all over each other in the limo driving back to the hotel. I was in the lucky middle. I had the attentions of Tia and Brandon. It was like they were fighting over me. I think it was Tia that first reached between my legs and started stroking my clit.

She poked around my panties under my skirt and fingered me while Brandon pulled me back into his arms and kissed me deeply. I stretched back into Brandon's lap while Tia reached between my legs, pushing my skirt up to reach the right place. Nothing like a woman knowing what another woman wants. She knew how to work me. Pleasure was her middle name.

She stroked slowly, kneading my clit between her fingers. Brandon took off my tank, and I felt the undressing begin. He cupped my breasts, circling the nipples while Tia slipped her fingers in and out of my moist opening. I was putty in their hands.

I opened my legs wider, letting Tia have full access as Brandon leaned back to watch. My eyes closed as I concentrated on Tia's rhythm stroking me into a frenzy. Again and again she was bringing me closer to the brink.

"Come for us Michelle. Be our sexy bitch." She moved faster, building me.

I breathed in as Brandon grabbed me and kneaded my tits. They built me up so high I felt I was going to jump off a cliff of pleasure. There was no turning back. I leaned back and gave myself to both of them. And I felt the crest of the wave take me over. I shuddered as they sent me over the edge. Spasms of pleasure rocked me, lulling me back into Brandon's arms.

Tia withdrew her finger, and sucked on the end. "I'd say your warm-up is complete." She climbed on top of me, my breasts pressed against her. Brandon was hard under my ass, growing harder by the second.

I teased in between my panting "I don't know if Brandon can handle all this."

"Are you kidding? I live for having this much action on my lap." He grabbed my breasts in a moving hand-bra.

"There are more ways to keep that lap full, Bran." Tia leaned over me, pulling off my skirt and panties. She began sucking on where she had been fingering before. I leaned into Brandon, his erection pushing against my back. The sandwich they'd put me in was turning me on in new ways.

Tia stopped, a teasing smile on her face. "But I can service you both. Double the pleasure. We just need to get Brandon ready."

I smiled at Tia, following her lead. I slid off Brandon, and helped Tia slide his black jeans off. He was so hard; he practically ripped off his own briefs as we began to slide them down. "No," I said. Let us do the work. A rockstar shouldn't work for his groupies."

"We work for you" Tia echoed my sentiments.

Together, we finished undressing Brandon and exposing his hot rockstar body. Everything was sculpted to a tee. His abs and pecs flexed as he lay back more on the limo seat. His shaved chest was caress-ready. He was a rockstar god.

"Now it's your turn to take your seat of honor Michelle. Slide next to your rockstar." Tia's voice held the hint of command.

I leaned up and slid onto him, slowly moving my body down his torso. A slick wetness kissed his stomach as I neared his hard cock. Tia moved up behind me, slowly removing her top and tight black pants. She wore no panties.

Tia did the same thing to me in the green room. She grabbed my hair, and pulled me back into a kiss. Brandon rested his hands on my hips, stroking my body to be a part of the female mounting. We had his cock surrounded. My ass cradled his shaft while Tia's mound pressed it against me.

"Can you fuck us both Brandon?" Tia grabbed the front of my breasts locking our bodies together.

"Never tried. I'll have to find out." He began moving his hips up and down, thrusting between our bodies. Tia leaned and angled behind me. I could feel the friction on my ass building the size of his cock. Then, Tia's hands took over, sliding up and down, slapping him against my back.

"Oh, girls. You know how to work me." His eyes closed in front of me. I watched his chest heaving to our ministrations. The beauty of his body responded to our prize catch of his trapped cock.

"I'm going to come." He caught up my hands. As I angled upward, Tia fed his long shaft into me. I stood up on my knees, taking in his full length, and rode him like a cowgirl. Back and forth, I built our passion, leaning as Tia cupped my breast, tweaking my nipples to build my frenzy like she knew how to do so well.

"Come in me Brandon" I pleaded with him. My need was growing so strong. He felt so good inside me. "It's my groupie's duty to receive you."

I leaned forward, pushing my clit against him. I felt the beginning of his erection spending itself within me. That triggered my muscles to contract around his shaft, having me join him in the orgasm. I moaned with Brandon as Tia moved down my stomach to finger my clit into a final peaking moment, and came hard.

We shuddered together, hands locked in mutual pleasure, and keeping my balance on the limo's couch like seat. I melted into him, lowering my body to his male model chest. My cheek leaned against his chest, and I didn't want to get off him. But time flies in a limo when having fun. The driver slowed as we bumped over speed bumps to get into the garage.

"I wonder if he could take those faster. You could rock me again like that. The both of you."

I kissed him as Tia said over my shoulder "I promise you. This is only the beginning to how fierce we're going to fuck you Brandon."

Chapter 3

It took us awhile to get dressed. This caused some attention at the drop off area in front of the hotel. They began to notice that a limo with someone had arrived. The bellhops came out of the hotel, followed by a few fans. Luckily, the darkened windows kept anyone from seeing the show of what we'd done to Brandon, and the dressing to get us back to public respectability. I knew my make-up was smeared in places I didn't want too obvious.

"Don't worry, Michelle" Tia laughed as she noticed me looking at my compact from my purse. "I don't think it's that noticeable from your face what you've been up to." She shoved on her pants angling half on the seat and the limo floor. "On the other hand, I'm sure my lipstick tells a whole other story."

Brandon laughed as he rezipped his jeans. "Actually, I wouldn't live up to my rockstarness if I didn't have messed-up groupies exiting from my limo. I've got a reputation to live up to, girls. Thank you for helping me with that."

He kissed Tia, and then me, lingering on my lips more than her. I caught a side-glance from her that spoke volumes. She looked jealous. But I couldn't tell which she was jealous of more, Brandon being with me, or me being with Brandon.

Tia opened the door, and Brandon followed. I came up next to him as he wrapped both of us into his arms. A groupie on either side was the way a rockstar should exit his limo into his hotel. There was a rush of people from the lobby when they recognized Brandon. He stopped for a moment, acknowledging the small group of people that came over to meet him. It didn't take long for objects to be signed by him to appear.

I tried not to look bored. I knew how important pleasing his fans meant to Brandon. Tia took the opportunity to get my full attention.

"You know, we could start without Brandon." She came up to me, leaning against me with her breasts. She caressed my jaw, looking into my eyes. I had to make a choice. I knew it would be cruel to lead her on. I really wanted to be with Brandon. Tia was hitting on me too hard to just want sex. I think she was thinking more than what I wanted to give.

"I'll just wait for him. I don't think it will take long." She seemed disappointed by my choice. She didn't lead onto it too much, but her pout told me volumes. I knew this might be a turning point so I added, "He's the biggest turn-on I've ever had."

I knew it hurt her from her face. Shit. But I couldn't lead her on. She was the additional turn on, but not my focus. "You're more like an extension to my foreplay Tia. I don't know how else to put it. You turn me on, but mostly when Brandon is around. You're like an auxiliary to our relationship."

She looked me directly in the eyes. "I see. You wouldn't want to do anything just with me?" Her eyebrow rose at her remark.

"No." There it was. Out in the open. I didn't want to hurt her. But it was the truth of my feelings. I owed her that.

"Okay. At least you're honest about it." She nuzzled up next to my face, caressing my cheek with her lips. She whispered, "If you should ever change your mind, honey, let me know."

At that moment, I watched over Tia's shoulder as Brandon turned and walked over. I pulled Tia closer, and gave her a small, lasting kiss. She'd done a lot for me in the last few weeks. There was something there. But not as much as there was with Brandon.

Brandon walked up behind her, and looked us over. I wasn't sure what he made us out to be. But he now looked jealous. Damn. What was going on tonight?

"You girls ready to go up?" He held the questioning tone while looking at me. He looked worried.

Tia spoke first, but didn't look at him "I think I'll wait a bit down here." She turned to Brandon. "After all, there are more people I'd like to see tonight. I think I'll go see what Randy is doing." She started moving over to the bar where Randy was sitting at with two other new groupies. One was the big-breasted girl Brandon had signed earlier. I saw his eyes follow her as she walked over. I was hoping he wouldn't follow.

He turned to look back at me. "And you, Michelle? What do you want to do?"

"I want to be with you Brandon. Only you. I want to rock you solo from now on."

He came up to me, wrapping his arms around my waist. His lips rustled against mine. We breathed in each other's air before pressing gently together in a deep kiss. I began taking in his mouth as if I needed him to live. I felt he was blending into me. His embrace took me closer, and we melted into one another.

When we moved apart, he wouldn't let go of my gaze. His eyes yearned for me. "I've wanted just you for three weeks now."

I felt intense relief and breathed outward. Then, I smiled. "Take me solo, Brandon."

He caressed my jaw, and traced down my neck while looking deep into my eyes. I was entranced by him, what he'd do with me all to himself. "Let's go upstairs."

Rockin' Him Solo

Hot Groupies Series Book 4

"I want to be with you Brandon. Only you," I whispered in the ear of Brandon Arturo, the lead singer of Sweet Fire. We were standing in the lobby of the hotel after the Sweet Fire show. Brandon had just asked me up to his room for a solo performance. I couldn't believe it. I'd been sharing him with other groupies in sexual romps that I could never tell my future grandchildren. He was staring at my eyes, a hair's breadth away from me. "I want to rock you solo from now on."

"With pleasure." He pushed me up against the wall as we waited for the elevator, wrapping his arms around my waist. His lips nuzzled against mine. We breathed in each other's air before pressing gently together in a deep kiss. I began taking in his mouth as if I needed him to live. His lower lip felt good to suck on. I felt electricity shoot through me as we connected again. I felt he was blending into me. His embrace took me closer, and we melted into one another.

When we moved apart, he wouldn't let go of my gaze. His eyes yearned for me. "I've wanted just you for the last three weeks now."

I felt intense relief and breathed outward. Then I smiled. "Take me solo, Brandon."

He caressed my jaw and traced down my neck while looking deep into my eyes. I was entranced by him, what he'd do with me all to himself. "Let's go upstairs."

I couldn't believe he wanted just me. Brandon Arturo, the hot lead singer of Sweet Fire, wanted to be with me tonight. Just me. I'd just rocked him in the limo with another hot groupie friend, Tia. But after three weeks of encounters with him and other girls, I wanted to be with him. Just me. Solo. And he had finally agreed.

His grin split his face. He bent slowly, nuzzling my lips before kissing me. This was different, more sensual. More personal. Grabbing my hand, he pulled me in the elevator, and pushed the button. Whipping me into a spin, he pulled me into his arms and kissed me again. I was drowning in kisses, and didn't want him to stop. All I could think of was him. No Tia. No Shelley. I could rock him by myself, as many times as I wanted. And I wanted to all night long.

The beep of the elevator stopped our kiss for a moment. He backed me into the elevator, and hit the button several times to get the doors to close. Before they did, two girls jumped into the car. The doors closed before anything could be done.

"What are you two doing here?" His eyebrow went up as he looked at them while he wrapped his arms around me.

"We're stalking you Brandon." One girl giggled as the other smiled next to her. "We want to be groupies."

"I don't think you two could handle him." I tried not to put too much snark into my voice.

But Brandon laughed at my answer. He pulled me closer to him, and started nibbling my neck. He spoke in between nibbles, "Sorry ladies. I'm taken already. I'm going solo tonight."

They both broke into a pout. "But we're you're number-one fans."

"And I'd like to keep it that way. Which floor, ladies?"

One girl looked at the other, then said "Seven."

He let me go for a moment to hit the button for the seventh floor, and the elevator started to move.

One of the girls pulled out her phone. "Can we at least get a picture with you?"

"Sure." He stepped over to stand between them.

I said, "Would you like me to take it?"

The girl handed me her phone. "Yeah. Sure."

He grabbed each girl around the shoulders, and they stood on either side of him in unison. They both gave him a quick kiss on his cheeks. I took the picture and the elevator doors opened as I handed the girl her phone. She walked out of the elevator saying, "Thanks Brandon. We'll never forget this."

"No problem," he said as the girls left the elevator. As the doors closed, he reached into his pocket, grabbed out a keycard and inserted it. "Can't get on our floor without the key." He hit the button for floor twelve and shoved the key card back into his pants pocket.

As the elevator started to move, he grabbed my hand and slowly pulled me toward him. "Now, where were we?"

Bliss. His lips were the largest, most succulent part of his body, and he knew how to use them. Our mouths couldn't let go as we tried to take the other being into ourselves. Moments later, the doors opened, and we broke apart. "Let's take this inside."

This time, I grabbed his hand. "What's your room number?"

"Suite 1214."

I pulled him out of the elevator and started down the hall. I reached the end, and followed the arrows that pointed to the direction of his room.

"Damn woman, you're in a hurry."

I started to rush ahead. "Good cardio will only get us in shape for what's ahead."

"We've been getting each other in shape for the last several weeks." He walked faster to catch up.

"Expect this to be one hell of a workout. I'm a brutal exercise coach," I said as we power walked next to each other.

"God, I hope so." He caught up with me and pushed me up against the wall near his suite. We were nose to nose, looking into each other's eyes. "Michelle, you mean more to me than a groupie."

"What do you mean, Brandon?"

His arms had me trapped, his body pushed up against mine. "I mean, these last few weeks is the first time…" he stopped and eased closer. His lips and mouth breathed into mine. "It's the first time I've considered anybody being with me on a more permanent basis."

"W-What do you mean?" I stuttered in response.

"You. Me. More permanent. What would you say to becoming my girlfriend?"

"Holy shit. Are you serious?"

"Deadly." He kissed me, pulling my body towards him. I could feel the hardness of his need for me. I moved against him, feeling his jeans rough against me. I grinded against him as he lowered his hands to my hip, holding me against him.

I wrapped my arms around his neck. "Is this real?"

"Say yes Michelle."

I looked at him. His muscular jaw was accented by a five o'clock shadow. A lock of his curly, dark hair fell into his eyes. His kissable lips begged for an answer. I kissed him.

He felt my answer and moved his hands to my back, pulling me closer. He grabbed my bottom lip in his mouth, sucking deeply before moving his tongue along the upper. I felt his hands move on my back, to the small of my back, and down on my hips. We were blending into one being.

When we came up for air, I leaned back laughing "I guess you understand that as a yes."

He started nuzzling down my neck, his lips tracing a searing fire trail. I tried to concentrate on making a suggestion. "Should we go in the room?"

He kissed my chin. "Eventually. We'll make it there." He moved to kissing my neck, and I didn't care where he did this to me, as long as he kept kissing. But I wanted more. I started to unbutton his black dress shirt, the one he'd been wearing to perform. I slipped my hands under the cotton fabric to caress his chest. God, I loved the feel of his naked skin under my fingertips. All mine.

"Maybe we should take this inside?" I suggested again, and laughed as he grabbed his keycard and shoved it in the door slot.

We were a tangle of limbs as we stepped into the room, closed the door, and somehow kept our bodies interlocked. I kissed him as he closed the door with his foot. Our feet slid under our joined bodies, and we shuffled near the bed. My hands went to unbuttoning the rest of the buttons on his shirt. I wanted to feel his chest underneath, moving beneath my caresses.

I pushed it back off his shoulders just as he reached under my top. I raised my arms so he could pull off the cotton top, and he dropped it to the floor. Finally, my breasts smashed up against his hard chest. I leaned into him, and we lost our balance and fell on the bed. Laughing, we didn't stop, but kept removing the layers from our bodies.

First, I sat up and unzipped my skirt. He leaned back, his arms under his head. I slid the skirt down my body and onto the floor. Then, I stalked him like a cat, slowly crawling on him. My nipples perked at attention. I arched my back before easing down the cotton panties I was wearing, the only thing separating me from his shaft beneath his black jeans. Lowering myself on him, I leaned over him, kissing up his torso until our eyes met. He wrapped his arms around me and pulled me closer. I could feel our hearts beating. This time, I could feel it was different.

It was just us.

His kisses were slower, luscious, pulling on my lips, as if he was enjoying the sensations of my mouth. I wanted to taste all of him. His skin was warm and sweaty, but with his scent. It was driving me crazy, the musky man scent wafting at me.

He kissed me and held me close suddenly. "Of all the nights we've been together, we're taking this one slow."

I leaned back for a moment, feeling my eyebrows go up. "Why?"

His voice got low and husky. "Because the other times we had sex. Tonight, I want to make love to you."

His words melted my heart. I caressed his face. "I want to make love to you too."

He pulled me close again, holding me tighter than ever before. Our mouths locked, but this time, there was more drive and passion. I couldn't get enough of him. I felt his hands moving all over my back. Our breathing became panting. He rolled to be on top, and moved up. He put his fingertip to my lips. "I want to make you scream my name, Michelle. I want to hear you say you want me."

"I want you Brandon. More than ever." I ran my fingers through his dark, glossy hair. "I've always wanted you."

He kissed me again, and moved down my body, slipping my panties down my legs. I could feel the air hit my wet slit. He reached between my legs, moving his finger between my swollen lips. "You're wet for me already."

"I've been wet for you all evening, Brandon."

His voice went low and seductive. "Tonight, I want this to be for you." He leaned down and drove his tongue into me. The thrust made me gasp, and he moved his tongue over my clit back and forth building me. My breathing turned to a rasp. I closed my eyes, feeling the sensations he built in me making me climb to my peak of passion. He moved his finger in me while flicking with his tongue. I was building so fast, I didn't know if I could stop.

He lifted his head, moving his finger faster and faster. "Come for me, Michelle. I want to see you."

His fingers worked their magic, flicking over my clit, moving to bring me to the edge. I felt the release that shook my whole body.

"You're sexy when you come Michelle. It makes me want you more." He moved back over me, kissing me again.

I could taste myself on his lips. I whispered, "I want you inside me. Make love to me, Brandon."

He answered me by sitting up and unzipping his pants. He slid them off, and I sat up to help him take off his briefs. We kissed, holding each other on the bed. Leaning me back against the covers, he finished sliding his briefs off. I reached for his shaft.

He grabbed a packet out of his jeans pocket, and I grabbed it from him. "Let me have the honors." I took the condom out of the packet and rolled down his length. I continued rubbing him, up and down, feeling his large length. Rubbing the tip with my thumb, I lay back slowly, pulling him by his member with me. I heard him growl. I spread my legs and guided him to my wet slit.

I moved my arms on either side of me. He braced his hands on either side, his large chest covering me. I felt safe and wanted. I wrapped my arms around his back. I felt his shaft tease the entrance of my pussy.
Slowly, he pushed, easing into me. He kissed my forehead, my cheek. Each thrust was gentle, loving. I closed my eyes and let Brandon plunge deeper. His lips met mine as he filled me so completely. My insides wanted to hold onto him, keep him this way forever.

He started slowly driving into me, pumping me into a frenzy. I met him with my hips, thrusting my body to meet his. Again and again, we united ourselves. My heart filled with the rhythm of just us. His eyes looked at me, and that's when I saw it. His need. We shared the feeling.

I kissed him as tears started to spring from my eyes. He thrust into me once more, and I felt him tense as my orgasm peaked. I came as I felt him shudder with me. Together, we rushed to the edge and over the cliff, falling hard into each other's arms with passion.

We lay together. He was still inside me. He moved next to me, and I snuggled into his chest. He whispered, "I've been meaning to ask you to come back to LA with me."

I was stunned. "What do you mean?"

He wrapped his arms around me. I could still feel him inside me. I knew that soon he would slip out. I moved closer, enjoying this connection. He spoke again. "I've been thinking about you an awful lot during this last part of the tour. We're finishing up in the next week. After that, I want to see you more that you're my girlfriend."

My heart skipped. "So, this is real? I'm not imagining this."

His voice was low and sexy. I could think of all his songs in this voice, when he sang of the women he loved. "I'll fly you out."

I blinked. "I still have to go back for finals. My friends have been taking notes for me which should help me through the exams. Finals will take a week or so, and then," I caressed his cheek, "I'm all yours."

"Then, when the semester is over, come stay with me. You can even stay for the summer, if you want." He moved, and I could feel him slip out of me. I immediately wanted him back inside me. He moved his body on top. He must have felt the loss too. "Stay with me for the summer. I've only got a few festivals planned, and I have a whole album to record. I want you by my side as I do that." He kissed me, his lips trying to make me see things his way.

It wasn't hard. I wanted to be with him. "For the summer."

His sexy whisper enticed me again into another kiss. "Be my muse."

He leaned over my body. His chest sheltered me. I wanted to stay with him like this. I wasn't sure if it would be forever, but I would take the now. "Yes."

His smile made me laugh. He kissed me so hard that it made me want him to make love to me all over again. "We can do this all summer long."

I laughed. "Yes. Solo. I like it the best."

"Yes. It sometimes takes just that one woman to get me off the ménage scene for a bit." He caressed my hair and nuzzled my neck.

I laughed as I grabbed him around the neck. "Or just one hot groupie."

"The hottest groupie. Mine, now." He kissed me again, and I was lost in that kiss.

He was mine. Finally.

About The Author

Just when you thought it was safe to go out at night, I arrive on the scene. Greetings darling. I'm **Lynda Belle**. I've always been with you, stalking you when you go to sleep at night. I'm part of your subconscious. I'm the naughty part that wants to come alive with fantasies that would make your mother blush.

I write erotic romances for women that want to forget reality and explore their secret, dirty love. I'm here to take you to those places. I've been hard at work writing new adult erotic stories to arouse you to new levels of erotic fantasy. Join me for some dirty love.

For more information on Lynda Belle:

Amazon Author's Page:
https://www.amazon.com/author/lyndabelle

Twitter: https://twitter.com/Lynda_Belle

Website/Blog: http://lyndabelle.com

Newsletter: http://eepul.com/bdhOr5

Acknowledgments

I'd like to thank all of the erotica writers on Kboards.com. Your tips have been invaluable. Lisa and Alain, thanks for being able to take on this project at the last minute. You totally Queen Latifah'ed it. Claudette, thanks for the editing eye you turn onto my manuscripts. You know how to crack all my projects into shape. And to all of you, my readers. You keep me going to pound out story after story. This is all for you.

If you enjoyed this book, please feel free to express your opinion in a review on Amazon or Goodreads. I would appreciate the feedback.
-Lynda Belle

Other hot erotic tales by Lynda Belle:

Scottish Erotic Tales:
Highlander Bride Taken
Highlander Bride Seduction
Highlander Bride Freedom

Vampire Pleasures Series
Bordello of Vampire Pleasure #1
Bordello of Vampire Pleasure #2

Bordello of Vampire Pleasure #3

On Call Series:
The Perfect Escort:
The Perfect Date

Exhibitionists Encounters Series
The Day I Met Her
The Night I Met Him

***All ebooks are Kindle Unlimited titles.

**Soon to be available as omnibus print editions.

www.ingramcontent.com/pod-product-compliance
Lightning Source LLC
Chambersburg PA
CBHW071628140626
46555CB00021B/1253